Brave Dave
And
The Time Goblin

By
Simon Woodward
Illustrated by Ralph Platt

This book is copyright. Subject to statutory exception and to provisions of relevant collective licensing agreements, no part of this publication may be reproduced without the prior written permission of the author.

In this work of fiction, the characters, the places and events are either the product of the author's imagination or they are used entirely fictitiously. Any resemblance to actual persons, sentient beings, living or dead is purely coincidental.

For Molly and Tilly, my daughters

Special thanks go to Sophie Evans, William Irwin and Ben Tuffs for their comments and general guidance.

I also have to thank my wife, Yve, for her patience and ability to read and read again the ever-developing story of Brave Dave and Tariq.

And finally I have to thank Mark Allen for proofreading a genre that is not part of his regular reading regime.

To all of these people I mention I am truly indebted.

Chapter 1. Tariq's Soup and Door Knocking _____ *1*

Chapter 2. Lettuce Camouflage _____ *11*

Chapter 3. The Problem with Wind _____ *23*

Chapter 4. In the Lab _____ *33*

Chapter 5. Nightmares _____ *47*

Chapter 6. Olive Oil and Cement _____ *53*

Chapter 7. Concretonator Away _____ *69*

Chapter 8. Enjoyable Exercise (not) _____ *77*

Chapter 9. A New Problem _____ *83*

Chapter 10. Blinkin' Dog _____ *87*

Chapter 11. The Observatory _____ *105*

Chapter 12. Trevor Emit _____ *107*

Chapter 13. Morning Was Broken and Goggle ___ *113*

Chapter 14. Lettuce Custard _____ *129*

Chapter 15. Little Green Man _____ 134

Chapter 16. Smelly Air _____ 143

Chapter 17. The Problem with Time Goblins ____ 149

Chapter 18. Dog Flaps and Clocks _____ 163

Chapter 19. Breaking Time_____ 171

Chapter 20. Gas _____ 185

Chapter 21. Dogs Don't Like Rubble_____ 195

Chapter 22. No Problem _____ 199

About the Author _____ 203

Chapter 1.
Tariq's Soup and Door Knocking

Tariq settled down for the evening, happy that his life had got back to normal after the strange meeting with the feather in a skin-tight yellow Lycra bodysuit; a feather whose name was Dave.

His thoughts turned to the Tortoise Tall Story Talkathon; an event which was going to take place in about five or six months' time. He couldn't wait to meet up with his friends and tell them about the strange day he'd had. He was sure they would wonder in disbelief as he told them about the amazingly weird feather from the sky; a feather that liked to be called Dave.

He was proud to go to the Talkathon and looking forward to it, especially as his mates had given him the title *'Tariq The Gifted of the Insomniacs'*, although this version of his title wasn't quite the title he'd really been given. All that his tortoise friends had named him was *'Tariq of the Insomniacs'* as he had a sleep problem. However, Tariq being Tariq had ignored that fact and added the words *'the gifted'* to the title himself and what a great title it was.

***

Tariq got up from his sofa and walked across his hutch to the kitchen area, then started preparing his meal for the evening.

Opening a cupboard he took a lettuce from its shelf and started peeling the leaves from it, dropping them one by one into some boiling water; he had started making his most excellent, hot 'n' soggy, lettuce leaf soup.

This was just one of the culinary delights he was most expert at cooking; or so he liked to think.

Taking some apples from his fridge and dumping them into the smoothie maker, he made his preferred drink; there really was nothing better than hot 'n' soggy lettuce soup washed down with an apple smoothie.

He wondered whether he should write a lettuce soup cookbook and one day appear on the telly.

"You never know," he muttered to himself, smiling at the thought.

Sitting back down on his sofa, whilst he waited for his soup to cook, he opened the local evening newspaper, the Daily Heron; which had just been popped through his letter box.

To Tariq's surprise, there was a photo on page two he recognised and although it was very blurry and in black and white he knew instantly it was a photo of the strange person he had said goodbye to that morning; it was Dave, a strange sort, if ever he had met one.

The story went on to describe how a short and brown looking individual, wearing a bright yellow Lycra body suit, had caused havoc in a house just up the road and then had promptly disappeared without trace!

Poor chap, Tariq thought to himself. *He's had it, he won't be able to go anywhere without being recognised now. If he's really lucky not everyone will believe what's written in the paper.*

Tariq's lettuce leaves were coming to the boil so he put down his newspaper and went over to the cooker to turn it off, then laid the table for dinner.

Tariq knew he was going to enjoy this immensely, especially as he was the expert at lettuce soup.

Standing at the cooker he decided to have a quick taste and after a few spoonfuls he expertly spat it back into the saucepan, deciding it needed a little more seasoning.

Just tremendous, he thought and went off to his pantry.

Picking the pepper and chilli ketchup from the shelf and then going back to his cooker, he added the new ingredient to the soup.

After some vigorous stirring, he put the soup back on the cooker and waited for it to heat up again. Once the soup had started to boil he removed the saucepan and poured himself out a portion.

Sitting back down at the table he took another sip of his delicious recipe and for the second time he spat the soup out.

Ah yes, Tariq thought. *I've forgotten the croutons.*

He went back to his kitchenette, opened the bread bin, took out a loaf of bread, cut a slice off and put it in the microwave for ten minutes.

While the slice of bread was being turned into something that was crouton like he spread out his food preparation cloth.

PING, went the microwave.

Tariq quickly removed the slice of bread and placed it in the centre of his crouton preparation cloth. Once done he folded the edges of the cloth over the microwaved slice.

CRUNCH.

Tariq slammed his crouton mallet down as hard as he could onto his cloth-covered microwaved bread, shattering its contents.

Wandering back to the table he emptied the cloth into his bowl of hot 'n' soggy lettuce soup.

At last he could have his meal. Tariq supped a huge spoon's worth and jumped back from the table dismayed.

"Eerrr... gazpacho, tremendous!" There was one thing that Tariq *really* didn't like, nor even wanted to get used to, and that was cold soup.

Picking up his bowl he put it back on the cooker. Hopefully, this would be the last time he'd have to heat it up.

THUMP, THUMP, THUMP, went the door to his hutch.

"Don't even think it Tariq," Shell shouted.

Shell was Tariq's imaginary friend, someone he had dreamed up to chat with over the lonely and cold winter months while he waited for the spring to arrive and along with it, his tortoise friends.

He had been doing this so long now Shell had become almost real, and she never failed to speak her mind. There was no getting away from her. She was Shell, his shell, and he had to live with the fact.

Chapter 2.
Lettuce Camouflage

Tariq steadied himself heeding Shell's warning.

"Wh... who's there?" Tariq warbled.

"It's me..., Dave," Dave shouted through the door.

"Dave?..., Dave is that you?"

"Yes, I just said it was... Is that you Tariq?" Dave said, getting his own back.

"Yes...," Tariq said, becoming confused.

"Tariq the Gifted of the Insomniacs?" Dave continued.

"Yes," Tariq said once again.

"Thought so," said Dave.

"Hey, Dave, come on in," Tariq said a little surprised at the return of the strange feather.

"Can't," Dave said.

"Can't?" Tariq asked.

"Yep," Dave agreed, "I can't," he said again.

"Why not?"

"You need to open the door," Dave explained.

"Oh... that. Just slide the bolt."

"Can't."

"Why not?" said Tariq.

"You've put your sign back up."

"What sign?"

"The sign that says '*For Tariq's use only. In case of emergencies*'."

"Oh yeah," Tariq said remembering and made his way to the door to open it. "Dave... well, well, well."

"Yes, thanks, thanks, thanks. Are you?" Dave said.

"What?" Tariq said frowning.

"Well," said Dave.

"Yes," Tariq said still not sure what was happening.

"Well, well, well," said Dave.

"What?"

"Oh nothing. Good to see you again, Tariq."

"Actually, Dave, it's good to see you again."

"You won't believe what happened to me today," Dave said.

"Won't I?" Tariq said and before Dave could respond Tariq continued, "Come in, Dave. Have a seat, sit down," Dave entered Tariq's hutch and sat down on his tatty brown leather sofa.

Dave stared silently at Tariq. Tariq looked back at Dave.

"Well?" said Tariq.

"Thought you'd never ask Tariq," said Dave, and began to tell Tariq about his adventure.

Enthralled, Tariq sat and listened to Dave's story only butting in once to ask him what he meant by the *concrete causeway*. Dave described the long flat hard thing which lay between two grass strips in front of the house he'd gone to.

"Oh you mean the road."

"Do I?" Dave asked, not ever having any experience of roads before.

"Of course you do," Tariq said.

"Alright then, the road," Dave continued his story. When he got to the bit about the apparition, its eyes and the pitch fork, Tariq started to quiver and shake, this part of the story was not making him feel very happy about anything, especially as night had fallen.

"Blimey! You did all that? Well there's one thing extra I know about you now, Dave."

"What's that?" Dave asked.

"You're the bravest feather I have ever known. Admittedly, the only feather I have ever known but brave nonetheless."

"I wouldn't call it brave," Dave said. "It was something I just had to do."

BANG... KERCHINK...CHING, CHING, CHING.

Tariq disappeared into his shell trying not to disturb her too much on the way.

"O," went Dave cut off in mid-Oh. "Clop," Dave continued.

Silence descended.

A few moments went by, and Tariq popped one eye out of the top of his shell for a quick look around.

"Aaaaaarrgghhhhh," Tariq screamed. "Dave..., Dave, what was that?..., Dave you've turned green. Daavveee," Tariq finished, popping his eye back into his shell.

"Blop," Dave replied then continuing in a low moan, "ooooooooooohhhhhh," Adding finally, "ow, ow, ow", when he'd managed to clear his mouth of green goo.

After a short pause Tariq popped his whole head out of his shell and looked about his room.

Tariq was instantly drawn towards his front door where an almost flat circular silvery addition to its surface could be seen sticking out from it.

"FLYING SAUCERS!" squealed Tariq. "No," he added, quickly changing his mind with a huge sigh of relief. "Flying saucepan lid... Phew — Dave what happened to you?" Tariq said, noticing that Dave was now completely green.

"Oh... nothing really. I just decided to explode and following that I decided to remove my lettuce-leaf camouflage suit which, fortunately, I had with me in a concealed pocket, and then I put it on for your pleasure and I did all this whilst swallowing part of the suit for my final trick."

"Really?" Tariq said, extremely impressed.

"NO! Not really you daft tortoise. Some idiot left a pan of boiling lettuce on the cooker." Dave licked his lips, "with added chilli, tomato and..." Dave licked a lump of an old soggy crouton from the corner of his eye, stating finally, "and bread."

"Oh," said Tariq, sheepishly. He had forgotten about his most excellent culinary delight, the one which he was going to write cook books about.

Tariq looked at Dave just in time to see Dave attempt the delicate extraction of lettuce leaf bits from his right ear.

"Sorry," Tariq said.

"Don't look," Dave said.

"Why?"

"Just don't. OK?"

"OK," said Tariq, popping his head back into his shell.

Dave stood up and started the sacred wet dirt removal dance. All the green goo slid off into a puddle on the floor. Dave stepped out of the puddle and sat back down on the sofa looking as fresh as the day he had been shed.

"OK. You can look now," he said.

Tariq popped his head out of his shell now that he had been allowed.

"How did you do that?" Tariq was intrigued.

"Don't worry about that, it's a secret," Dave said.

Chapter 3.
The Problem with Wind

"Go on, Dave, tell me the rest," Tariq prompted.

Dave went on to tell Tariq about how he had managed to thwart the apparition's attempts to move the pencil case and how a horrible rotting green hand had appeared from nowhere to zap the apparition into oblivion.

"So that's what happened to me," Dave finished.

"Wow," Tariq was truly amazed. This story would definitely go down well at the Tortoise Tall Story Talkathon.

"There's one thing that still bothers me about the whole adventure though," Dave said.

"What's that?" Tariq asked.

"Why on earth do I keep being lifted from the ground this way and that by some force I cannot see."

"You're a feather," Tariq explained, albeit not very well.

"Really?" Dave said sarcastically, as if he didn't know *what* he was.

"Yes really."

"I know that. But what's that got to do with the price of fish?"

"Nothing. But you're as light as air, or should be."

"And?" Dave said.

"It's wind."

"I beg your pardon." Dave sniffed, nope nothing was going on there.

"No. Wind, air wind," Tariq said sensing Dave's embarrassment.

"Air wind," Dave thought about this concept. "OK tell me more," Dave said not entirely sure what Tariq was going on about.

"Movements of air created by differences between areas of high pressure and areas of low pressure, in the atmosphere," Tariq said.

"Low pressure and high pressure" Dave repeated trying to get the idea straight in his head. "Let's see if I've got this right." Dave continued; "What you're saying is that differences in air thickness, with high pressure being thicker air and low pressure being thinner air, causes the stuff the air is made of, to move from the thicker air in the direction of the thinner air, and it's these movements that make me move?"

"Yep," Tariq said, sighing with relief.

"Doesn't fit with what happened to me. There wasn't any of this wind today."

"Ah... Now you're talking induced pressure."

"Induced pressure?" Dave queried, confused about his problem again.

"Yep, the pushing of air, say by an apparition, from one place to another making the air left behind, after the pushing, a lot thinner; a gap in the air if you will. It is that gap that has to be filled with air that is not as thin, that is; the thicker air around the gap," Tariq explained.

"So when the air moves from where it is to where it isn't any more, then this creates air movement, and it is that movement which moves me around, as if I didn't have anything else better to do," Dave finished.

"Exactly," said Tariq.

"Why?" Dave asked.

"Because you're a feather," Tariq said.

"Yes... I know that. But what's that got to do with the price of fish?"

"Nothing. But you're as light as air." Tariq stopped and looked at Dave feeling that the whole conversation was going to be totally pointless.

Dave was smiling. "Sorry Tariq. I do get it really," he said.

"Good," Tariq responded, not impressed one bit.

"But how am I going to get around this problem. It's not very helpful when I'm trying to do good and great deeds, as it is my destiny to do. For I am the helper of all living things and without my destiny, I have nothing, nobody to help and no reason to be."

"Believe it or not I've already thought about that, Dave," Tariq said.

"You have?" Dave said stunned.

"Yep."

"How?" Dave responded.

"A machine."

"A machine?" Dave questioned.

"Yes — a machine," Tariq continued. "One that will increase your weight so that air will treat you with the respect it treats concrete."

"And what way would that be?" Dave asked.

"Heavier," Tariq said quite seriously. "I, Tariq," he prattled on, "will build this machine for you. This machine will be unlike any other ever created before. A machine that will give you powers of the like never seen or felt on this plane. The machine will be known as the *Concretonator*."

"The *Concretonator*?" Dave repeated. "Aren't you getting a bit carried away?"

"No. There is one thing I know for sure, and that is this; concrete is heavier than air."

"Everyone knows that," Dave said.

"I know, but not everyone has that power, the power to make air treat you just as it treats concrete."

"And how, exactly, is that?" Dave replied.

"NOT AT ALL!!!" Tariq said slowly, saying each and every word carefully and individually.

Dave could almost hear the drum rolls.

"OK. Let's do it," he said.

Chapter 4.
In the Lab

"Follow me," Tariq said to Dave, leading him to the back of his hutch.

At the back, there was a dirty rug hanging on the wall. Tariq pulled it to one side revealing a door.

"Is that going to help me?" Dave said looking at the newly revealed door.

"No," Tariq replied, "But it is what is behind this door that will help you."

Dave just stared at Tariq, wondering what could possibly be behind the door that would help him.

Tariq pushed open the door and a staircase into the ground below Tariq's hutch, came into view.

"A staircase?" Dave observed trying to work out how some steps would help him get over his problem with the wind.

"Not just any staircase, Dave," Tariq said. "But steps into a special place; a place where I create all my inventions."

"Oh!" said Dave.

Tariq reached into the passageway and flicked a switch. A single bulb on a wire hanging from the ceiling above the stairs lit up the dingy wooden stairwell.

"Come with me," Tariq said in a low and ominous tone.

They both descended the dimly lit stairs. Once at the bottom Tariq flicked on another light switch illuminating a huge box-like cave, carved from the soil below Tariq's hutch.

Dave looked at the dank room noticing all kinds of mechanical bits and pieces stacked on the shelves and on the floor.

"What d'you think?" Tariq asked.

"Well," Dave said, "it's a brown dank room with lots of bits of machinery and other stuff."

"Not quite," Tariq said. "This is my laboratory. This is where I do all my experiments during the winter; designing machines and creating exotic food dishes, such as hot 'n' soggy lettuce soup."

"Really?" Dave said.

"Yes," said Tariq with utmost sincerity. "And this is where we will build the *Concretonator*."

Dave was not certain about this proposal. *How can someone*, he thought, *who cannot boil lettuce successfully, be relied upon to devise and then create a machine like the Concretonator? Oh well*, he sighed to himself.

"OK," said Dave. "Where do we start?" Dave felt this was probably not the right thing to say, but hey, let's give the guy a chance.

Tariq wandered to the back of the lab opening a drawer and pulled out a huge piece of paper with all sorts of diagrams on it.

"When did you start designing this thing?" Dave asked becoming very curious. It was obvious to him that there was no way Tariq could have known of his up and coming re-appearance at his front door.

"A long time ago, but this design is not exactly the design of the *Concretonator*. It is just something I was working on in order to give Shell a chance for a holiday, without me. The machine was designed to give me an artificial shell while she was away, but I never got around to finishing it."

"Who's Shell?" Dave said.

Tariq, not wanting to be thought of as slightly mad, ignored the question and carried on. "Well, as I see it, you need a *shell* of sorts; something you can wear to stop the problem you have with the wind."

"I don't have a problem with wind, Tariq, thank you very much. It's air wind," Dave said.

"OK. I understand what you're saying, Dave," Tariq said. "Now, all I need to do is change the design so that when the machine's turned on it works to your size."

For the next couple of hours Tariq took Dave through the machine's design describing the parts, they would need to build the *Concretonator* and once finished they started the work.

Dave and Tariq rummaged through the lab pulling the necessary bits and pieces from the shelves, dumping them all in the middle of the lab's floor.

A tumbler out of a tumble dryer, the inner tubes of bicycle tyres, motors from food mixers, big vats from ice cream vans, pots of glue, a bag of cement, some canisters of cod liver oil, a remote control for a DVD player, the insides of an old computer and finally a hose.

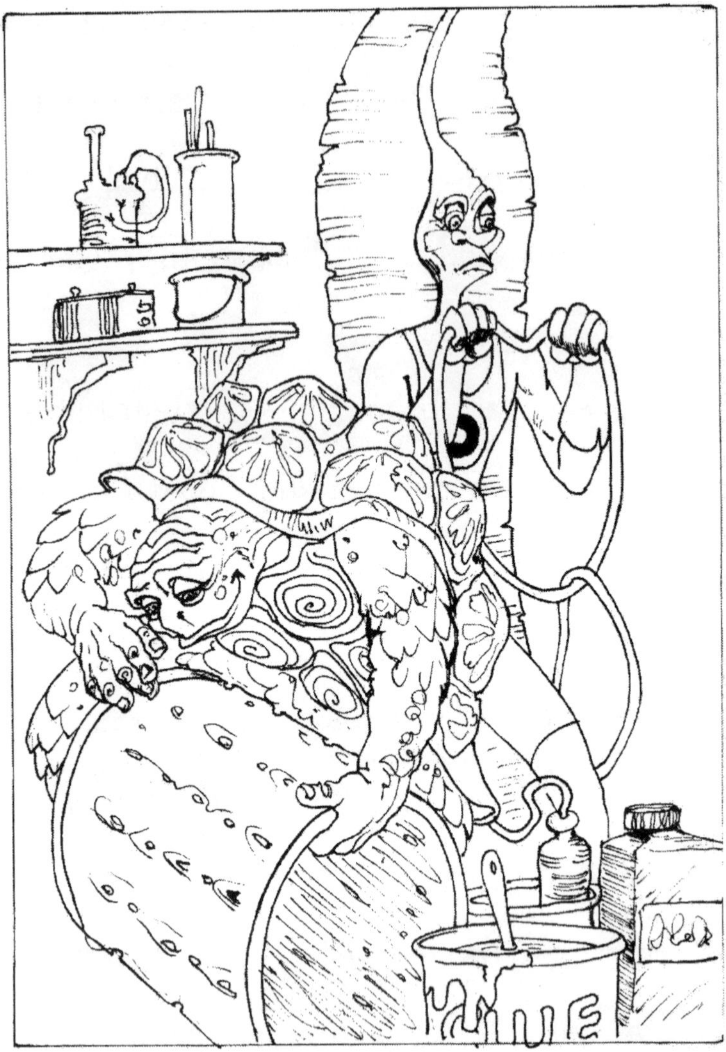
GLUE

When they'd finished Tariq declared with some glee, "We're ready to start building the *Concretonator*."

"Have you ever built a machine from one of your designs ever before?" Dave asked.

"Yes... sort of... no... I suppose not," Tariq said. "I haven't really had the time, what with the creation of the most excellent culinary delight."

"And what was that?"

"Hot 'n' Soggy lettuce soup with chilli tomatoes," Tariq said.

"Surely it couldn't have taken that long?" Dave asked.

"Dave, to get these things absolutely right does take some time you know."

"How long?" Dave said.

"About six years," replied Tariq.

"Six years!" Dave said stunned. "For a soup? — A soup you still haven't got the hang of?"

"To get such things right takes time you know," Tariq repeated.

"OK. So what you're saying is that you've never ever, ever, built a machine you have designed, ever before, because you were working on making soup?"

"Yep. That's about the long and short of it," Tariq said.

"And you don't see any problems at all with what we're trying to do?" Dave asked.

"Nope. Why should I?"

"No reason, just wondered." Dave was becoming very worried about the whole project. However, he dismissed his worries; he knew that if he was to fulfil his destiny then something had to be done about his wind problem. Not being able to see any other way to make the situation right, Tariq's machine would have to do.

Dave decided to go with the flow. What's the worst that could happen? He wondered.

Tariq pulled an old stainless steel, food preparation table from the depths of his lab. "This will be the chassis," he stated.

Picking bits of machinery from the middle of Tariq's lab's floor they both got to work.

First they manoeuvered the vat from the ice cream van and placed it on to the top of the steel table.

Tariq crossed the lab and opened his tool box, lifting out a huge drill. After plugging it into a wall socket Tariq drilled a few holes in the ice cream container and then sliced up the hose and bicycle inner tubes with a pair of garden shears, attaching them to the fledgling machine.

Working busily, Dave and Tariq continued to add the other bits and pieces from the lab floor to the table and ice cream container.

By four o'clock in the morning Tariq declared that the machine was complete.

Dave looked at it astounded. It did seem rather impressive, but it hadn't been turned on yet. Dave decided he would wait until the machine had been shown to work in the way it had been designed to before helping Tariq any further.

"I'm tired Tariq. What else is there to do?" Dave said.

"Not much. You go upstairs and get some sleep. I'll add the final touches," Tariq said; still full of energy and with no sign of fatigue or tiredness.

Dave wandered back up the dingy wooden stairs into Tariq's hutch and aimed straight for the very comfortable looking bed. He was asleep almost before his head hit the pillow.

Chapter 5.
Nightmares

Dave was dreaming about his past. The life before he had been set free. He was back with his crowd of other feathers flying over the English Channel, and he was happy.

Gradually, the journey towards France got worse and more unpleasant; there was an incredible amount of turbulence, the air had become terribly bumpy, so much so that he was finding it very difficult to keep Jonesy, his father, his creator of sorts, up in the air.

The next thing Dave knew they were all heading straight down, head first, towards the sea with no land in sight.

Jonesy didn't seem to be that bothered but Dave, or Seventh of Nine Thousand, Three Hundred and Forty Two (feathers), as he used to be known, sometimes Seventh for short, knew they were in terrible trouble.

Jonesy could not float, let alone swim, because poor old deluded Jonesy was a buzzard and not a swan as he had thought, and definitely not aquatic as the orphaned Jonesy had assumed from a very early age, though he'd never dipped so much as a claw into a river or stream.

Jonesy hit the water and after some surprise at the new knowledge he did not have any idea about swimming, or even staying afloat on water successfully, for that matter, poor old Jonesy started to sink.

Seventh and his colleagues were being dragged under the sea, not able to breathe and not able to get airborne again. Water was rushing around them, soaking them, making them heavy as they didn't have the special waxy coating "normal" water birds had on their feathers.

Seventh blinked trying to understand what was going on.

"Hoob berberler." He heard as he went under the surface. "Ber ber her ber ler hayve," the noise continued as Seventh sank deeper and deeper beneath the waves.

"Hayve hake hup ber ber ler," the strange voice went on.

Dave blinked, *Turtles?*, he thought. *I'm truly sinking*.

"Dave, wake up," Tariq said, concerned, as he gently tried to shake Dave awake, "I think you may be having a dream,"

Tariq decided that he was probably better off with the problem of not being able to sleep, especially if dreams made you feel like this.

Dave opened his eyes and saw Tariq, then sighed with relief, but the relief was only temporary.

"Dave, it's morning, and the machine is completed. It's time to test it." Tariq was extremely excited. Dave was now even more concerned than he had been during his horrible dream.

Chapter 6.
Olive Oil and Cement

After a cup of tea Dave began to feel a bit more like his new self. He followed Tariq back down into the lab.

"What's in there?" Dave said pointing to a huge container of grey, oily looking slurry, which was sitting on top of the stainless steel food preparation table.

"That's what your shell will be made of," Tariq said.

"Yes. But, what's in there?" Dave continued his questioning.

"Well, it is a particularly, delicately, balanced emulsion, a mixture of very, very, very small lumps in liquid. Sort of like paint but not, solely designed to give you a comfortable freedom of movement. The shell will form around you when the emulsion has been ejected from the *Concretonator*."

"Tariq, just tell me what's in there. OK?" Dave said concerned about what was probably going to happen next.

"Olive oil and — cement," Tariq replied, giving up on the idea of keeping the ingredients of Dave's shell suit from him.

"OLIVE OIL? AND CEMENT?" Dave repeated, exasperated.

"Don't worry," Tariq said. "It's been specially formulated," he finished, thinking his last statement would make Dave feel calm and comfortable with the answer.

"You have got to be kidding."

"Honestly, Dave, it's OK. Trust me, I'm a tortoise."

"AND?" Dave said, not feeling any reason whatsoever to accept Tariq's explanation.

"Dave, it is far better to trust and be disappointed in a tortoise than to distrust and be disappointed in strife," Tariq said answering Dave's question.

"What's that supposed to mean?" Dave said.

"I don't know, but it's probably relevant."

After a few moments thought Dave sighed a huge sigh. "OK Tariq what do I do now?"

"Right. Go over there," Tariq said pointing, "and stand in that specially constructed cabinet."

"You mean that old shower cubicle?"

"Yes, but it's a specially constructed old shower cubicle," Tariq said to Dave, trying to get across the idea that the cabinet had been specially constructed.

Dave wandered over to the cubicle and got in it, then asked, "What do I do now?"

"Nothing. Just put on those eye protectors," Tariq said pointing at the goggles hanging up in the cabinet, "and hold your arms out horizontally,"

Tariq picked up the *Concretonator*'s plug and pushed it into a vacant power socket on the wall, pressing the on switch.

The food mixer's motors, which were now part of the *Concretonator*, whirred into life and the '*specially formulated*' olive oil and cement slurry started to circulate around the ice cream vat.

Tariq strolled back to his machine and unclipped the hose from its side, pointing it at Dave.

What am I doing? Dave thought to himself.

"Ready, Dave?" Tariq asked.

"I suppose so," Dave said reluctantly.

"Arms out then," Tariq commanded; then started his count down. "Five, four, three, two, one. *Concretonator* away," Tariq twisted the valve, which he'd attached to the end of the hose on his *Concretonator* machine, and out shot a jet of yellowy grey mixture.

Dave felt the impact from the jet of slurry directly on his chest as the mixture covered him.

Tariq turned up the pressure and the increased force sent Dave smashing through the back of the cabinet only for him to be halted by the wall behind it. Dave was now some five metres away from the cabinet and at least one metre above the floor.

"SSTTOOPPPPPPP," screamed Dave.

"What's that, Dave? I can't hear you," Tariq shouted, trying to be heard over the noise of the *Concretonator*.

"BLOBBBB, BLOP, BLOBBB," Dave said, his mouth completely covered by the *Concretonator*'s thick liquid.

"Sorry, Dave," Tariq shouted again, still trying to be heard over the noise his machine was making. "I still can't hear you," he said. "I'm going to have to turn the machine off. Is that OK?" Tariq said finishing his yelling.

"YOB," was the only answer Dave was able to give him.

Tariq closed the hose's valve and wandered back to the wall socket and turned off the power. The noise died away.

Tariq looked at his cabinet.

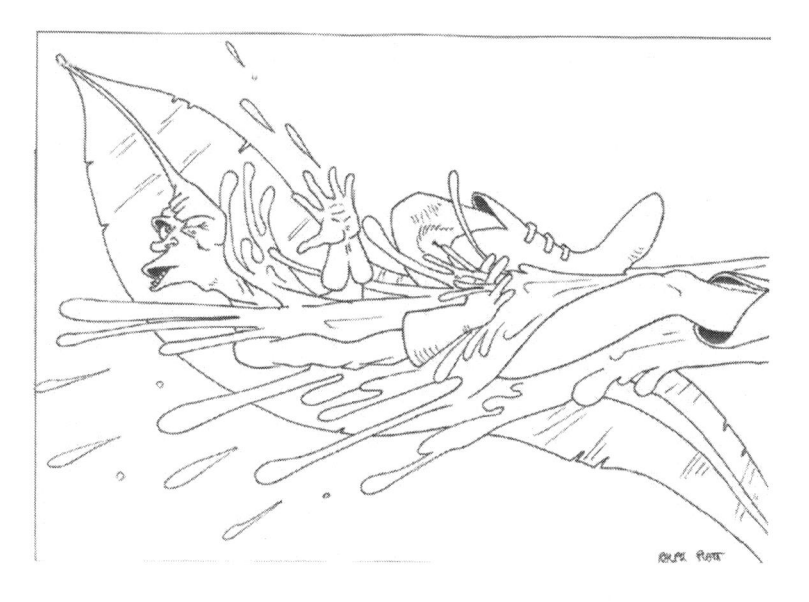

"Oh," said Tariq, as he noticed Dave was no longer in the cabinet and somehow a huge hole had appeared in the back of it.

Tariq walked up to the cabinet and looked at the hole, poking his head through it. Then he looked at the wall behind.

Tariq noticed the wall had gained a yellowy dark grey blob which was gradually getting lighter as it dried.

"Ah!... You OK, Dave?" Tariq said.

The yellowy light grey lump gradually peeled away from the wall head first, then crashed to the floor smashing into pieces.

Dave pulled himself out of the now shattered hardened slurry, shaking his left arm as he did so trying to get rid of a particularly stubborn lump of concrete which had stuck fast.

"What are you trying to do to me Tariq? Kill me?" Dave said, still trying to shake another hardened lump of slurry from his other arm, "Look," he continued, pointing at his left arm.

"I think I need to reduce the power in the motors," Tariq said. "What do you think, Dave?"

"What do *I* think? — I think you're mad. That's what I think," Dave said in a huff.

"Come on, Dave, calm down, it was only the first test. You can't expect things to go perfectly first time. Now be reasonable."

"Calm down? Reasonable? First test!?"

"Yes. I mean, you're not a giver-upper are you?" Tariq said.

Unfortunately for Dave there was only one answer he could give to this question.

"No," Dave sighed, beaten.

"Right. All I have to do now is reduce the power and modify the emulsion slightly. Then we'll be ready to go again once I have repaired the cabinet. Why don't you put the kettle on?"

"OK," Dave said. He was beginning to understand why he had been extremely concerned in the first place. Dave left the lab and made his way up the stairs to Tariq's kitchenette, and put the kettle on.

Dave knew he had to carry on with this experiment as there was really no other way, he could see, to get over his wind problem.

Tariq retrieved the *Concretonator* design from the drawer and examined it intensely once more.

He was certain that he had missed something, but was not quite sure what it was. An hour later Tariq understood the error.

Ah! The current mixture is not flexible enough. He thought to himself. *What I need is something to make it more rubbery*.

Tariq looked around his lab and all he could see were some spare car tyres.

Right, Tariq said to himself thinking. He ran up the stairs to his kitchen.

"Hi, Dave," Tariq said as he entered the main area of his hutch.

"Oh... Hi," Dave said

"Not ready yet, but I will be soon," Tariq enthused.

"That's really fantastic Tariq. Really?" Dave asked.

"Yep," Tariq said, "Don't you think this is tremendous?"

Oh great. Dave sighed inwardly, not bothering to answer.

Tariq opened the kitchen cupboard and pulled out a food blender and a bottle of stain remover then shut the cupboard door, opened another and took out a box of unused mothballs then rushed them all back down to his lab.

Dave didn't have a clue what was going on. He was only certain that this would mean more testing and that he would have to be a part of it.

***

Tariq plugged the food blender into the nearest socket taking off its lid. He then cut bits from the car tyres and put them into the blender. Once it was half full he replaced the lid and turned the blender on.

The food blender began to judder, but as the tyre clippings were gradually shredded into smaller pieces it steadied itself.

When the blender was steady Tariq added the mothballs and after the usual juddering the food blender contained a powdered mixture of car tyre and mothballs. Tariq then poured the stain remover into the mixture and turned the food blender back on once more. A few minutes later Tariq was left with a slimy rubbery solution. Taking this to the *Concretonator*'s tank he added it to the remaining cement and olive oil slurry.

Ever the perfectionist, Tariq attached a DVD remote control to the *Concretonator*. He was now certain that it would allow him to adjust the mixture and the direction of the flow as and when it was necessary.

Chapter 7.
Concretonator Away

"Dave," Tariq called up the stairs, "we're ready. Come down."

Oh no. Dave thought, "I'm on my way," he said.

"I'm glad you're here, Dave" Tariq said. "I've finally sorted out all the problems and there is nothing for you to worry about now. Just go and stand in the cabinet, which I specially constructed, and you will be able to see that everything has been set right."

"Fantastic," Dave replied, not meaning it one bit as he trundled himself off to the cabinet and got in it.

The hole in the back of cabinet had been repaired with a sheet of MDF, the medium density fibreboard being glued and nailed in place.

"Wait there, Dave, I'm now adjusting the direction and force." Tariq was fiddling with the DVD remote which was now the only way the machine could be controlled. The *Concretonator*'s nozzle was quickly moving left and right, up and down as Tariq pressed different buttons.

"I'm ready, Dave" Tariq said.

"OK," Dave replied, knowing that this maybe his last appearance in the world.

"Right" said Tariq, "Five, four, three, two, one, *Concretonator* away!" Tariq pressed the red button on the machine's newly added controller. The hose spewed out its contents spraying the ceiling; before swinging sideways and spraying the shelves then the nozzle changed direction again, spraying the far end of the laboratory. Finally it stopped.

Dave's eyes were wide open along with his mouth; he couldn't believe what he had just seen.

"Whoops," said Tariq, "Wrong button. Sorry, Dave. I could never get the hang of these controls. Just stay there. I'll get it right in a minute."

Dave stood still; trying not to look worried, as Tariq attempted to work out his new control system.

"Stay where you are, Dave. I think I've got the hang of it now," Tariq called over to Dave across the lab.

Dave was trying to stop his knees knocking.

Tariq pressed a green button; the *Concretonator* aimed directly at Dave and a thick liquid splurged out from the end of the nozzle.

Dave had already taken a deep breath as a precaution, but this time the gooey stream exerted little or no pressure on his body at all.

Tariq was jumping around whooping with joy very slowly. This was a first. He had actually made something that worked and after all this time perhaps he could be like his grandfather Tarquin.

"This is absolutely tremendous," Tariq exclaimed joyously.

Dave looked at his body; it was now covered in a thick slimy liquid which was extremely flexible, almost flexible enough not to cause any problems with his movement. He could move his arms, he could move his feet and he could look from side to side. Dave took one step out of the cubicle and after an initial resistance to gravity he fell flat on his face.

"Dave, are you OK? How are you feeling?" Tariq asked.

"Probably yes, and very heavy," Dave answered in order.

"OK. That's to be expected," said Tariq. "Can you move?"

Dave tried moving his arm, his arm did move fluently but slowly which was quite good for a feather being completely covered in some kind of rubbery cement.

Dave tried moving his foot and he found that it also moved. Dave tried to lift his head up from the floor and he was able to do that as well, with only a little struggle.

Dave was surprised his new coating (or suit) was flexible, he could move even though the mixture was heavier than he was used to.

"Right, Dave. It is obvious that you can move but at this moment in time you are finding it a bit difficult... so I think you need some training," Tariq observed.

"Yep, I think you're right Tariq," Dave said, struggling to stand up.

Dave's new shell suit was amazing, every direction he tried to move he could, albeit with some resistance. He would definitely need to do some serious training in order to wear the suit without issue. But he knew now that his wind problem was over; finished.

"OK Tariq, what do I do next?" Dave said.

"Dave, I will create a training plan, a plan never devised before and together we will get you used to your new shell suit and I'll show you exactly how. Right?" Tariq said.

"Absolutely," replied Dave, feeling a lot less worried than he had earlier.

Chapter 8.
Enjoyable Exercise (not)

Tariq had set up a training circuit along the back wall of his underground laboratory.

"Right, Dave, while you have your new shell suit on you'll have to build up your strength so you can move easily when you're wearing it."

"OK. What's the next step?" Dave said.

Tariq explained to Dave about the training circuit. "...and that's all you have to do," Tariq finished.

Dave looked at the apparatus and frowned.

What have I let myself in for now? He wondered. There, in front of him, were benches, parallel bars and a treadmill.

Following Tariq's instructions Dave started the circuit. He walked across the benches, struggled across the parallel bars and ran on the treadmill. Then he ran up and down the benches and heaved himself back across the parallel bars and jogged on the treadmill once again.

After one hundred circuits around the tortuous assault course Dave collapsed on the floor.

"Enough," Dave begged.

"OK, Dave," Tariq said, "You can stop for five minutes, but I must say that four hours is not really enough."

"Not enough?" Dave exclaimed.

"No, and for one reason only."

"That being?" Dave wheezed.

"That being the fact that you will, more likely than not, be wearing your tremendous shell suit for a lot longer than four hours, when you need it."

"OK. I get your drift. How long then?" Dave said.

"I reckon, probably... another five days ought to do it," Tariq replied.

"Another five days?" Dave repeated, utterly stunned at Tariq's answer, and now very, very worried.

"Yep. That's how long," Tariq stated in his matter of fact tone.

Oh my god, Dave thought to himself. *I'm going to die.*

"Don't worry, Dave. You won't die," Tariq reassured him. "Trust me, I'm a tortoise."

Five days later a very exhausted Dave begged breathlessly, "Can I have a cup of tea now?"

"Of course you can," Tariq said, "You've completed your training."

Dave struggled out of the rubberised concrete shell suit and wandered back up to Tariq's kitchenette and before you could say *'circuit training for five days non-stop is extremely exhausting'*, Dave was sound asleep on Tariq's sofa yet again.

Chapter 9.
A New Problem

"Dave I've found it."

Dave gradually opened his eyes, all the while trying to ignore the silent burning screams which were now coming from his arms and legs.

"Ay?" Dave asked, trying to hear Tariq over the din of his muscles.

"I've found it," Tariq repeated.

"Found what?"

"Your next adventure, the task that your new shell suit was designed to help you with," Tariq said.

"And what's that then?" Dave said.

"This. Have a look," Tariq showed Dave the two page feature in the most recent Daily Heron.

"What's that got to do with anything? I mean it's only about the Emit family and the fact that they've been entered in to the Guinness Book of Records for being the world's worst ever time keepers," Dave said.

"Yes, but don't you find their circumstances rather strange?"

Dave re-read the Daily Heron's article. "What? The fact that they do not have any jobs, the fact that they've never been able to go on holiday, the fact that their milk, which is delivered to their doorstep everyday, is always sour when they pick it up?"

"Yes," Tariq said.

"No," Dave finished.

"Honestly, Dave, if there is nothing strange then surely they would all be dead by now. And they look so reasonable," Tariq said looking at the Emit family picture on the second page of the Daily Heron feature. The picture consisted of the Emit family and their unhappy looking dog.

"Ok. Now you've said that, it does seem slightly strange," Dave agreed.

"I think this is a case for Brave Dave the Feather and Tremendous Tariq the Tortoise; the gifted tortoise that is," Tariq said feeling masterful.

Oh no. Dave sighed inwardly for the millionth time that day.

"OK Tariq what do we do now?" he said.

"Easy," Tariq replied, "we pack up and get round to their house as soon as possible."

Chapter 10.
Blinkin' Dog

Dave and Tariq got their stuff ready and put Dave's shell suit on to a small trolley. There was no way Dave could wear the suit all the way to Trevor Emit's house, wherever that was, the suit was too heavy.

After phoning the Daily Heron Tariq managed to get the newspaper to reveal the road the Emit's lived in, but unfortunately not the house number.

However, Tariq had decided that this was not a problem and they would go to the road anyway; then take it from there.

Tariq was sure the Emit's house could be found without any issue and Dave would resolve Trevor Emit's problem because Dave was Brave Dave the Feather, helper of all needful people and in this case, Trevor Emit.

Dave was not entirely sure that Trevor Emit actually had a problem, but he decided to go along with Tariq's idea just in case.

"Ready, Dave? Know what we're doing?" Tariq asked.

"I think so," Dave replied.

"Good," said Tariq, looking forward to sorting out Trevor Emit's problem with Dave and being part of the adventure this time.

***

Tariq, happy in the knowledge that he knew what they were doing led Dave to the road. Dave followed, dragging the trolley which now contained his shell suit, behind him.

Making their way along the road Dave and Tariq failed to notice a big furry cat sitting in a tree watching them suspiciously and as it turned its head to follow their progress the morning sun glinted off its name tag reflecting the words '*my name is Slime*'; Slime was not only watching them, Slime was franticly scribbling notes into an old battered jotter.

***

After a while they reached the Emit's road and stopped for a breather. Actually Tariq stopped because Dave was puffed out; he had been pulling the trolley all the way.

"Tariq," Dave said grateful for the short break, "How will we find the Emit's house?"

"Well," said Tariq, "I am certain there will be something which will show us where the house is and when that something happens we'll know."

"Like what?" Dave asked

Before Tariq could answer a shaggy, short, unkempt white and ginger spotted dog scampered out of a drive way and came to a halt in front of them, looking confused.

"Hi dog," Tariq said, winking at Dave. The dog's eye twitched nervously.

"Do you know where the Emit's family house is?" The dog blinked then flicked its head to one side and blinked again.

"Dave," said Tariq, "I think this dog has got a nervous tic."

"That I have," said the dog overhearing Tariq's comment, all the while continuing to blink uncontrollably while flicking its head and occasionally trying to scratch its ear with one of its rear legs.

"Dave, did you hear that?"

"What?" said Dave.

"'*That I have.*'" Tariq repeated.

"Yep. Why? Didn't you?"

"Of course I did. But what was it?" Tariq said.

"The dog you fool," Dave replied.

"Wow! A dog that talks," Tariq said.

"What's so amazing about a dog that talks?" Dave asked.

"It's a dog," said Tariq.

"Yeah, and you're a tortoise," Dave pointed out.

"So?" Tariq questioned.

"You talk," Dave said.

"Right, but it's a dog!" Tariq replied.

"I know. And you're a tortoise," Dave said again.

"Are you trying to say that I am the same as a dog?" Tariq said, a little put out by Dave's comment.

"No, of course not, Tariq," Dave said, "But you are a quadruped. You are an animal with four legs," he finished.

"Right," said Tariq.

"Right," Dave said.

"Right... OK. Do you think there is any mileage in asking it where the Emit's house is?"

"I don't know," Dave said, continuing, "Why did you ask it in the first place then?"

"Because I thought it might point," Tariq replied.

"Point?" Dave asked, not sure what Tariq was trying to say.

"Yeah. I can see that's not reasonable now, especially as it can't stand still for one moment."

"Well," said Dave, "Ask it again and see if you get an answer."

"Dog," said Tariq, addressing the dog once more, "do you know where the Emit's family home is?"

"I do know of the Emit family's home," the dog answered.

"That's tremendous," said Tariq. "Are you alright?" he continued, getting distracted by the dog's twitching.

"What do you mean?" said the dog.

"I mean, are you alright? You seem to have a problem," Tariq carried on.

"I don't have a problem. Do you?"

"No," Tariq responded quickly, not quite sure why he had been asked this.

"Why do you think I have a problem then?" the dog asked collapsing on the floor and vigorously scratching its exposed stomach with its other rear leg, which wasn't quite enough so the remaining rear leg joined the first one in the scratching.

"Because you just can't keep still," Tariq replied, adding, "Actually, you cannot even keep upright."

"That's not me," the dog continued, getting up from the floor still blinking and twitching its head. "That's my tick. It's very nervous you see."

"No, not really," Tariq said.

"Well," said the dog, "I have this nervous tick."

"Yeah," said Tariq, "I can see that."

"But you don't," said the dog.

"Yes I do," Tariq countered.

"No you don't," said the dog again.

"OK. Explain it to me."

"I have a nervous tick. One that you cannot see," the dog explained.

Tariq looked at Dave shrugging his shoulders and shaking his head smirking. How on earth could the dog say that he, Tariq, could not possibly see the nervous tic?

"But I can," Tariq said to the dog.

"No you can't," said the dog again, "I have a tick that is nervous."

"Eh?" Tariq said slipping into confused mode.

"The tick I have" the dog continued, "being a tick, an arthropod if you will, happens to be one of a nervous disposition. It is the nervous disposition of the tick which makes me twitch."

"Ah! You have a tic," Tariq repeated still convinced that the dog was going on about a nervous affliction.

"Exactly," said the dog, believing the tortoise had finally got it.

"A tic that is not a twitch but an Arthur Pod," Tariq said attempting to clarify (mainly to himself) not daring to delve into a dictionary and make himself out to be uneducated, because he was. (Educated that is). Anyway Arthur was certainly a stupid name for a pod especially as a pod was the name for a bunch of dolphins. What on earth was this dog trying to say? That it had a whole gang of dolphins roaming about its body and the gang's name was Arthur? How stupid.

"Got it in one," the dog replied, a bit happier.

"A tic that is nervous?" queried Tariq.

"Yes," said the dog.

"Why is it nervous?" Tariq asked.

"Don't ask me; ask It," the dog said.

"Where is it?" Tariq said, not knowing why because he could certainly see that the tic was all over the dog.

"If I knew that then do you really think I would allow it to stay about my person?" the dog said.

Tariq was caught out by this question so he turned to Dave. "Dave?" Tariq said hoping for some help.

"Personally, I don't think that a dog, in its right mind, would really want a tick on itself," Dave said.

"Right," said the dog. "Anything else you want to know?"

"Err. Yeah," said Tariq trying to put the tick question out of his head.

"And what may that be?" said the dog.

"Do you know where the Emit family home is?" Tariq tried again.

"That I do," said the dog.

Oh my god. Tariq sighed to himself. *Why can't anyone give me a straight answer in the first place*? "OK dog. Where is it?" he asked.

The dog pointed its nose at the house Tariq and Dave were now standing in front of.

"Thank you dog," said Tariq.

The dog wandered off in the direction of the Emit's house.

"Dog. Where are you going?" Tariq called after it.

"Home," said the dog.

"You live there?"

"Yes," said the dog, "I am the Emit family pet."

"Tremendous," Tariq said, exasperated.

Chapter 11.
The Observatory

"Dave, we're here," Tariq said.

"I know that Tariq. The dog just said so," Dave replied.

"Well, what do we do now? This is your specialist area."

"I think we need to sit and observe the situation to see if we can get an angle on the problem we believe exists," Dave said, adding to himself, *or at least the problem you believe exists*. "But before we sit down we must find a place to observe from."

Dave looked around the Emit's front garden and spotted a small opening in the hedge which lined a small brick wall separating the garden from the pavement. He wheeled his trolley into the hedge and signalled to Tariq. Tariq came over and joined him, the both of them sat down on the trolley and started their vigil, waiting and observing, to see what would happen next.

Chapter 12.
Trevor Emit

Trevor Emit was sitting on his lounge sofa smiling to himself. He was truly looking forward to the post's arrival the next day. This was it, he would get the job he had applied for and at long last he would be employed.

All he had to do now was to wait for the letter saying that he had got the job. This time he would succeed after all these years.

And perhaps his wife would be pleased. Daphne always said that she believed in him but how much longer would she wait?

He had promised her so much when they met but he had never been able to deliver on his promises, especially when the promises had required him to be at a certain place at a certain time.

Poor dear Daphne, it wasn't as if he hadn't been to university. It was only the fact that when he had got to the exam room to take the final exam he had found it empty, much like the lecture rooms he had gone to during his terms at Uni.

Even more than that the exam room doors were always locked; so it wasn't really his fault that he hadn't got his degree, it was more due to the fact that the examination was not on the day he had got there.

This trouble, the trouble of not being on time had haunted him for a large part of his life. No matter how hard he tried, nothing had worked; being on time was something he'd never been able to achieve. Could lateness be genetic? He didn't know but he certainly wished it were because then he could blame it on his parents, whoever they were; and he didn't know this because he had been orphaned at a very young age.

***

Trevor was very lucky to be married. It was only Daphne's belief in him that had allowed the marriage to go ahead.

When he hadn't turned up at the altar at the prescribed time, she had waited. Not only had she waited, she had waited three days, and when he had finally got to the church and made his way through the crowd which had gathered outside, Daphne had still been standing at the altar and still willing to marry him.

She hadn't cared about the other couples who had been queuing up, nor their guests, she had just believed in him.

But things were different now; it was six years later; six years of being married to the worst ever time keeper in history.

So bad was he that he now had an entry in the Guinness Book of Records, an entry under the most un-praiseworthy title of '*The World's Worst Ever Time Keeper*'.

Trevor had to do something; he didn't know what, as he believed he had tried every trick in the book; every single trick to make sure he was on time.

But it never worked. However he had faith and it was this faith in himself that had kept him going. How much longer would it keep Daphne going he didn't know.

Chapter 13.
Morning Was Broken and Goggle

Morning was breaking and it was 7:14am. Dave opened his eyes; he had been roused by the *click, click, click* of a bicycle freewheeling. It was the postman. Tariq was somewhere in his shell doing stuff and Dave did not bother to disturb him.

The postman rested his bicycle against the front wall of the house whose hedge Dave and Tariq were hidden in, and walked up the path to the front door.

Putting his hand into his postbag he pulled out a single letter and placed it in the letter box which was attached to the front of the house; it was one of those letter boxes which needed the owners of the house to leave their front door to collect their post.

The postman got back on his bike and cycled off to the next address requiring a delivery.

***

Trevor was woken from another strange dream about time pieces, clocks and other such things by his radio alarm clock. He opened his eyes and the dream began to fade away. As usual he was left with a feeling of almost understanding. This was one of the most frustrating things about waking up. He could never grasp what it was he was meant to understand. Shrugging the feeling off, he got up.

***

Outside Dave heard a quiet *thud, thud, thud*. It was Trevor coming down the stairs to collect his mail.

The dog, the one Dave and Tariq had encountered the day before, came out from the back of the house and wandered around to its front, as if to see whether Trevor would manage to get the letter.

Suddenly a strange looking individual popped out of a small drain in the Emit's front garden.

The dog started twitching and shaking, as if the tick had started the world's first ever Rave dance contest for arthropods on a mammal, which was crazy because arthropods had been doing these competitions for years.

The individual was short, no more than about thirty centimetres, dressed in green woollen clothing and wore a floppy pointy green hat. It was carrying what could only be described as a square wooden frame, not much larger than itself.

Dave was astounded by the appearance of the strange green man but was even more astounded at what happened next.

Just as Trevor opened the front door to his house, the peculiar individual held the wooden frame up to the door and as if by magic each side of the frame stretched until it matched the size of the house's door frame.

The view through the newly sized frame went all wobbly, it was as if Trevor was being seen through the surface of a murky green watery pool; one which had just had a stone thrown into it.

Dave continued to be astounded because all of a sudden the morning bird calls stopped and the sun zipped across the sky, faster than you could undo a pair of jeans, to take up its mid-afternoon position for the time of year.

Trevor opened the letter, read it, looked at his watch, and sighed heavily.

"No, no, no," Trevor moaned, "I was here, I got up at the right time. The letter says I can start work at 10:15am, for my first day. Nooooo," he finished.

"What time do you make it Tariq?" Dave whispered into Tariq's shell.

"About 1pm. Why?" came Tariq's echoing reply.

"No reason," Dave turned back towards the house because the phone in the house had started to ring. The strange green individual had disappeared and so had the dog.

Trevor picked up the phone.

"Mr Emit," the phone said.

"Yes," said Trevor.

"Don't bother coming in. You're fired."

Click, went the phone.

Trevor looked at the handset momentarily; then hanging his head he slowly replaced the phone's receiver, miserable.

"I don't know why I ever bother getting my hopes up," Trevor said to himself, closing the front door.

***

Dave spent the rest of the afternoon pondering over Mr Emit's problem. Nothing much else happened apart from a few muted yells coming from the house, followed by such statements as "*I've burnt the bloomin' potatoes again*," Which were promptly followed by responses such as "*Don't worry darling I'll do some more*," And apart from that, the house was quiet and there was no sign of the strange and short green man.

"I think Mr Emit has a problem," Dave said finally.

"I know that," said Tariq popping his head out of his shell, "That's why we're here. What is it?"

"Ah! Well. That is quite difficult to explain, but in essence I feel it's got something to do with time frames," Dave said. "One thing is for sure though, we'll not be able to do anything about it today."

"How come?" Tariq asked.

"We need to do some research. This is not a case of your everyday wannabe poltergeist problem," Dave said referring to the problem of the missing school books he had solved the other day. "Time to go back to your hutch I think," Dave finished.

It was now 6:21pm, the sun had just set, and Dave with his trolley, plus Tariq, made their way back to Tariq's hutch in the deepening twilight.

***

When they got there Dave plonked himself down on Tariq's sofa.

"Do you have a book on genealogy?" Dave asked Tariq.

"I think so. But why do you want a book on denim? Do you have a cunning plan where we create some kind of cotton travelling machine or perhaps a swing or even a wig?"

"No. No. No. I need to find out about Mr Trevor Emit's family tree," said Dave.

"Sorry, I thought you were asking about blue cotton clothing or something."

"I really don't know how you manage to achieve anything Tariq, genealogy not jeanieology you idiot."

"Ah. Well. That's something completely different. And I don't think I do. You could try using Goggle."

"Goggle?" Dave queried.

"Yeah, Goggle," Tariq said, "it's the '*Internet search engine that surfs the information sea with clarity*'," Tariq said quoting the website's marketing phrase. "A search engine that will see exactly what you need to know."

"Internet? Search Engine? What are you going on about Tariq?" Dave said, asking about these new things he had not heard of before.

"Well, perhaps I do know stuff then," Tariq said, feeling rather chuffed with himself.

"What is the Internet? And what on earth is a Search Engine?"

"Don't worry, Dave. I'll show you."

Tariq walked across his hutch and pressed a concealed button on the side of an old Edwardian writing desk. The desk front opened up and a keyboard slid out on a pair of black rails. The top of the writing desk then flicked back and a small screen rose silently up from inside it.

"This is my secret connection to the entire world," Tariq said.

"Wow," said Dave agog. "What's that?"

"It's a computer terminal. A terminal that allows me to look up things I don't have books about."

"OK, barring the fact that I have no clue as to what a computer terminal is, you've got me interested. Show me what it can do," Dave said.

"Ask me something... anything," Tariq said.

"OK. What is the base of the natural logarithm 'e'?" Dave smiled to himself knowing that there was no way that Goggle the '*Internet search engine that surfs the information sea with clarity*' could know this. And there was definitely no way Tariq would know this either.

In a short moment after tapping away at the keys of his computer terminal Tariq said, "2.71828182845904523560 blah, blah, blah."

"Bloody flip," Dave swore absolutely stunned. His mouth jabbered silently in awe. "Right. Right! Right," Dave eventually continued still not able to get over the power at Tariq's finger tips. This could be an extremely useful research tool, he thought.

Chapter 14.
Lettuce Custard

"OK, Dave, where do we go from here?" Tariq asked.

"I think there are a few essentials we need to know before we can have any hope of helping the Emit's, especially poor old Trevor," Dave said.

"What are they then?" Tariq asked.

"Well, firstly, we need to know what that little green man was about," Dave said, continuing, "secondly Trevor's family history is something else and thirdly, what happened to the morning."

"What little green man?" Tariq said not recalling any little green man at all.

"Oh...yeah, I forgot," Dave said, "What were you doing in your shell this morning anyway?"

"Ah... that is a question. I'm not sure I can tell you. It's a secret," But Tariq being Tariq couldn't keep it to himself.

"I have started developing the most excellent culinary addition to my hot 'n' soggy lettuce soup main course."

"Good for you Tariq. Can you tell me what it is?"

"I shouldn't, as I haven't got anywhere near completing the recipe but as it's you I'll tell you... Lettuce custard."

"Lettuce custard!" Dave repeated trying not to feel ill or give away any sign that he thought it was probably the most stupidest idea that Tariq had come up with so far after his hot 'n' soggy lettuce soup with microwaved bread.

"Yes. I'm just in the process of figuring out how to cook beetroot in order to add it as a topping, but haven't quite got there yet."

"That's good," said Dave, meaning that it was good that Tariq hadn't got around to finishing what could only be called the most awfulest recipe on earth. Dave hoped Tariq would never get around to finishing it because he knew that he would be the one who had to try it.

"Anyway, what little green man?" Tariq asked.

"Well, while you were working on your new recipe a little green man popped out of the drain with a wooden frame and moved time forward about five hours forty six minutes and thirty three seconds," Dave said.

"No? Really? You've got to be joking," Tariq said, finding it hard to believe what he was being told.

"No I'm not. And this is exactly why we need to do some proper research."

"Why? Because getting beetroot to be a good topping takes an incredible amount of in depth knowledge about root vegetables?" Tariq said.

"NO!" Dave said, "Because little green men from drains don't just happen as an everyday occurrence and therefore something really odd must be going on. Will you please focus on the Emit's problem and not your cooking. OK?"

"OK, ok. Don't lose your fancy yellow Lycra over-garment about this," Tariq said.

Chapter 15.
Little Green Man

"Tariq, what does Goggle say about little green men and floppy caps?"

Tariq typed the question into Goggle. "Dave, we've got a result."

"Excellent. What does it say?"

"It says '*Bombay, India. 1917. Informal group portrait of Australian troops, possibly a reinforcement for the 1st Wireless Signal Squadron, Mesopotamian Expeditionary Force, relaxing in the water.*' Does that help?"

"How do you expect that to help, you fool? I knew it; this Goggle is not all it's cracked up to be."

"I don't know why you asked me to do that anyway. I'm sure I've got an old book on little green men and such things."

"Well thanks for letting me know that Tariq. Where is it?"

"It's over there on that shelf, it's called, '*The Guild of Gaia's Who's Who of Magical Beings.*' I think that'll cover what you're after."

Dave walked over to the bookshelf and pulled off a very large and heavy dusty book opening it up. After a few moments of flicking through the pages Dave came across a picture he recognised.

"That's it Tariq, it's a Time Goblin! Well done that tortoise. Sometimes the junk you collect really does do the business," Dave was now excited about the prospect of solving the riddle of the green man.

"What's a Time Goblin when it's in a drain?" Tariq asked.

"Well according to the book a Time Goblin is *'a mythical being brought to life after the creation of Elves from the earth. After the Elves were made the remnants that were left were used to create the Time Goblins.'* Apparently, because they were made from what was left over after the Elves had been created, they have a long standing hatred of them. But, even more importantly, they also have a special hatred of mankind, mainly because mankind was the first creature to be created from the earth. It also says that *'Time Goblins were given certain powers'* one of those powers being *'the power to control time to compensate them for their outrage about how they were brought into being.'* And *'as part of their Quadalveus'*, which is basically their magic toolbox, they were given, *'An Emar-Femit'* which, roughly speaking, is a wooden frame which can control time but only on a very localised basis: amazing!"

Dave was happy now that the nature of the green individual had been identified: but one question still remained; why was the Time Goblin hassling poor old Trevor Emit in particular? To delve into this mystery Dave had to understand Trevor Emit's past.

"Tariq do you have a book on Genealogy and I don't mean a book of cloth swatches OK?"

"No."

"Oh, ok. How am I going to finish this research then?"

"Goggle?" Tariq replied hesitantly

"OK. I suppose it's our only option," Dave said.

"What do you want to know then?"

"The Emit family tree," Dave stated.

Tariq started to type away at his computer terminal. After a few exclamations of 'no', 'not this one', 'nope' Tariq finally said. "I think I've got it."

"Dave, have a look at this. I've found an Internet site called 'www.extremely-ancient-family-trees.org'. I think this will do the trick, mainly because it's extremely old."

"How can you tell that?"

"Well apart from the download times, which are extremely slow, just have a look for yourself."

"Wow," Dave said, "That looks really old," Commenting on the ever so visible cobwebs covering the web site.

"Yep. It certainly is,"

"OK. What do you do now?"

Tariq brushed off the cobwebs from the site.

"There, look, there's a place we can type names into. What I'll do now is enter the family name you want to research."

"OK enter '*Woodward*'."

"What? What's that got to do with anything?"

"Nothing, I was just making sure you're on the case. Try entering '*Emit*'."

Tariq typed Emit into the site's search then pressed the enter key on his terminal. The search results spoke for themselves.

"This is truly amazing Tariq. These entries go back centuries."

After going through each and every link Dave said, "I think we now have some idea of how we are going to sort out Trevor Emit's problem. Tomorrow we'll begin."

Chapter 16.
Smelly Air

Dave woke suddenly, something was really wrong. He sat up and looked for Tariq. He couldn't see him anywhere and this was partially due to the presence of a strange, very thick, and very smelly fog which was filling the room. It was also due to the fact that Tariq wasn't in the room either.

Noticing the fog was thicker towards the back of Tariq's hutch Dave decided that it must be coming from the rear, somewhere near the stair that led down to Tariq's lab.

Before going to investigate, Dave tied a handkerchief around his nose and mouth. Stumbling towards the door at the back the hutch holding his arms out in front of him Dave reached for the rug that covered the lab's entrance and pulling it back he stood aside as more fog billowed out from the stairwell.

"Tariq?" He called out, slightly muffled, because of the handkerchief he had tied around his face, and he definitely wasn't going to remove that.

There was no reply. Getting concerned over the lack of response Dave continued down the stairs, the dim light making the fog a light yellow in colour.

"Tariq?" Dave called again.

"Ah *dare* you are, Dave. How's it going?"

"What on earth is this fog?" Dave asked.

"Dave I like your handkerchief. Is that going to be *bart* of your *suberhero* look?"

"No and I'm not a superhero. What is this fog Tariq?"

"Don't worry, Dave. I've just *hab* by first go at creating Lettuce Custard but I *haben't* quite got it right yet," Tariq said.

"You can say that again," Dave said. "Is there anyway you can get some fresh air in here?"

"Why would I *wad* to do that?" Tariq replied.

"Because it stinks, actually it more than stinks, it reeks. No, no, reeks doesn't come anywhere near describing this smell. I don't think there is a word that could come anywhere near to describing it."

"Can't say I *doticed*," Tariq said.

"Not *doticed*? Have you got a cold or something?" Dave asked.

"*Doe*," Tariq replied, "I usually put a couple of these up by *dose* before I start *exberimenting* with *recibes*," Tariq showed Dave a spare set of tortoise nose bungs.

"And today?"

"*Yeb*!" Tariq confirmed.

"Blimey Tariq. Get some fresh air in here now," Dave rolled his eyes and thought, what is it with this tortoise?

Tariq walked over to his work bench and pressed a bright yellow button. The fog started to disappear into a small hole at the back of the lab.

"What's that?" Dave asked.

Tariq removed his nose bungs.

"It's an extractor fan, Dave."

"Why didn't you use that before?"

"Didn't want the noise to wake you," Tariq said.

"Did you ever think about the smell?" said Dave.

"What smell?"

Dave sighed.

Chapter 17.
The Problem with Time Goblins

"Come on Tariq, we really ought to get ready. I'd prefer to be at the Emit's place before dawn breaks."

It was still early in the morning.

Tariq's disaster with the Lettuce Custard had woken Dave around 5:30am. Sunrise was not due for another couple of hours.

Dave loaded his suit into the trolley and as an afterthought retrieved *The Guild of Gaia's,*

Who's who of Magical Beings' and threw it into the trolley as well.

Tariq picked up his satchel, stuffed a few bits and pieces into it, and slung it over his shoulder.

"OK, Dave I think I'm ready. Are you?"

"Yep, I believe so."

Dave and Tariq made their way out of Tariq's pen and on to the road and very soon they arrived at the Emit's home

"Tariq, I think we'll make camp where we were yesterday. Once we're done we'll work out a plan of action," Dave said.

"Great, I like action," Tariq said, trying not to show his apprehension.

He had never ever done anything brave before, apart from investigating the noise which had marked Dave's arrival in his pen. This time it was different, he was not in his pen and his hutch would be a long way away if things got a little scary.

"What's that knocking Tariq?" Dave asked.

"Don't know, Dave," said Tariq.

"It's your knees," Shell said to Tariq, for once not speaking out loud for all the world to hear.

Oh good grief, Tariq sighed to himself.

"What fleas Tariq. I don't have any fleas" Dave said not having any idea what Tariq was going on about.

"No, I said, I thought it might be the trees."

"I suppose it could be," Dave agreed.

Phew! Tariq thought and whispering quietly, "Shell keep your big mouth shut will you?" There was no response from Shell.

Dave and Tariq made camp under the hedge once again.

"What do we do now?" Tariq asked.

"Well, from the information we found out in the book and the information from the interesting net."

"Internet," Tariq corrected.

"OK, the Internet, it seems that the Emit family and the Time Goblins have been battling each other for all time. As far as I could work out the Emits, or at least, the Emit family line are here to defend normal time, to make sure that summer changes to autumn and autumn to winter and one year to another et cetera, et cetera.

"But the Time Goblins were given the ability to change time," Dave carried on repeating what he had read in the book, "in a small way; supposedly for the good, because if everything happened when it should then things would just be so tedious it was assumed that all living things would give up and die of boredom.

"So you have the Emits, and Trevor is just one of many throughout the world, a time guardian of sorts, and you have the Time Goblins. The Ying and Yang of time. A balance, not quite between good and evil, but more like between late and punctual."

"I see," Tariq said, "I think I know what you mean; every year when the '*Tortoise Tall Story Talkathon*' is on, it's meant to start at 8pm but no one actually turns up then. It's not until about 8:15pm when they arrive. And no one is actually late; it's more like they are on time."

"Exactly," said Dave.

"And this is due to the Time Goblins getting the better of the Emits?" Tariq said checking that he had understood everything so far.

"As I understand it, yes, but why Trevor has his problem I don't know. I'm sure his Mum and Dad knew their responsibilities and they must have brought him up to be a time guardian as much as they were."

"Strange," Tariq said, pretending to be thoughtful about this.

"Yes it is strange. We need to find out more and to do this we need to get in to the house."

"But he's in there with his wife," Tariq was getting seriously worried.

"I know, but I think there is a solution to that," Dave said and started to whistle. Tariq looked at Dave utterly dumbfounded.

KERLICK, CLICK, CLICK, CLICK, CLICK, CLICK.

The Emit's dog came skittering around the corner its toe nails tapping on the path as it went.

"Oh. It's you again," said the dog.

"Yep. It's us," Dave replied.

"What do you want?" the dog asked.

"I want to help you," Dave said.

"Help me?" The dog said, starting to twitch again, flicking its head this way and that. "What do I need help for?"

"I want to help you with your nervous tick," Dave said.

"Do I really have to go over that again?" Without waiting for a reply the dog turned around and started making its way back to the rear of the Emit's house.

"Hold on," said Dave quickly, "It's not strictly help for you. More like help for your tick."

"Help the tick?" the dog said not believing what it was hearing. "I don't think that tick needs any help. It's more than capable of giving me grief without any help from someone else."

"No," said Dave, "Help it not to be so nervous," he explained.

"And how might you do that then?" the dog said, curious.

"Well, I think I have worked out why it is so nervous."

The dog came back and Dave explained his theories. Dave then went on to explain what he wanted the dog to do.

"Your explanation is pretty far-fetched," said the dog, "Actually down right ludicrous. But as I don't have a feather's chance in a tornado to get this sorted out any other way, I'll do as you ask.

"Even if this does not work I suppose I am no worse off anyway," With his final comment the dog skittered back to the house.

"Tariq, get back under the hedge and get your stuff ready," Dave said.

"What's going on, Dave?"

"Wait and see," He replied.

A few moments later Dave and Tariq heard the muffled sounds of the Emits talking upstairs in their bedroom.

***

"Trevor, I think the dog wants to go out," Daphne said.

"Err?" said Trevor, sleepily.

"Trevor, the dog wants to go for a walk," his wife said once more.

Trevor looked at the clock next to the bed.

"Daphne it can't. It's only six in the morning," Trevor moaned.

"Trevor — I really think it needs to go for a walk. Look at it."

Trevor looked at the dog. It was running around in circles, at the bottom of their bed, chasing its tail and occasionally falling over.

"Yeah, I think you're right," Trevor said frowning slightly at the dog's strange and new behaviour. Getting up he got changed and started to wander down the stairs.

"Come on boy," Trevor called to the dog. "We're going for a walk."

The dog sat down in the Emit's bedroom looking at Daphne with its puppy eyes.

"Come on boy," Trevor called.

The dog didn't move.

Daphne pointed to herself and said "Me as well?"

The dog nodded.

"Trevor. I think it wants me to come as well."

"What has got into this dog? It's never behaved like this before."

"I don't know Trevor but even though it's early perhaps it would be nice, just this once, to go out before everyone else in the world is up."

Daphne got ready.

The dog jumped around wagging its tail eagerly and the Emits, now ready, took the dog for a walk.

Chapter 18.
Dog Flaps and Clocks

"Nice one, Dave. How did you do that?" Tariq said, seeing the Emits leave their house, following their dog.

"Oh. Don't Worry," And to himself, he added, *I just hope I'm right*.

Once the Emits were out of sight Dave and Tariq attempted the task of finding a way into the Emit's home and it couldn't have been simpler. Once they had got around to the back of the house Dave recognised the usual see-through flap. In this case it was a lot larger than the last one but it was a way in all the same.

"We go through there," Dave said pointing to the flap.

"Through there?" Tariq repeated, "Are you sure?"

"Of course I am," Dave said.

Dave and Tariq heaved themselves through the flap and landed in a room full of smaller doors.

"Ah," Tariq said, "we're in the kitchen."

"The kitchen? Yes I suppose it is but very much larger. Thanks Tariq you've made things a bit clearer."

Dave noticed the clock on the oven and said to himself, *Ah, there's one.*

"What do we do now then, Dave?"

"Well, as I see it, we need to remove every single clock in the house. Anything that has got to do with telling the time has got to go."

"Why, Dave?" Tariq asked.

"Because Trevor is a time guardian and instead of looking after time he has decided to be ruled by it. I don't know why yet, something in this house may just tell us. Anyway, Trevor just does not know he should be looking after time and not being dictated by it.

"And the Time Goblin, which lives in his drain, is stopping him from doing his job. Which funnily enough is exactly what the Time Goblin should be doing, but because Trevor doesn't know what he should be doing the Time Goblin is winning on every occasion.

"And it is this one and only fact that is unbalancing the time continuum around here and more importantly around Trevor's time.

"For us to undo this imbalance we need to remove anything that Trevor relies on to tell the time."

"And what exactly are we looking for?" Tariq asked.

"Well Tariq you could describe the problem in one word, clocks. Roughly speaking, anything that has hands on it that point to numbers," And as an afterthought Dave added "And anything with numbers on it that does not have hands."

"OK. And that's it?" Tariq said confirming what he had been told.

"Yes," Dave said. "So that we can cover the whole house as quickly as possible," Dave continued, "we'll need to split up. I'll take the upstairs and you can take the downstairs. When we find any kind of clock thing, it needs to be broken; made unfixable.

"I'll pile mine at the top of the stairs and you pile yours in this kitchen. Once we've finished we will dispose of them."

"OK. And to do this we'll split up?" Tariq asked, starting to get very worried at the prospect. Although Tariq liked to think he was as brave as Dave, he knew he wasn't.

"Yep. That OK?" Dave said.

"Of course it's OK. What do you think I am? Some kind of wuss?" Tariq said, pretending he wasn't.

"No of course I don't. Are you sure about what you need to do?"

"Absolutely, Dave. I'll start at the front of the house and work my way to the back. Where do we meet?"

"When we're finished we'll meet at this see-through flap thing," Dave said.

"Right. Off we go then?" Tariq said.

"Yep. Off we go," Dave said.

"How long do we have?" asked Tariq.

"Well, according to the dog, he can keep them out of here for at least an hour," Dave said.

"Is that enough time?"

"I hope it is and if we work fast enough then it should be," Dave said.

Dave quickly made his way up the stairs of the Emit's home.

Tariq made his way to the lounge, which was at the front of the house.

Chapter 19.
Breaking Time

Tariq had never ever felt this nervous, so scared and so worried in all his life before. This should be Dave's job, he thought, not his, but Tariq knew in his heart that there was no way Dave would be able to tackle this job on his own; especially in the time they had to complete it.

Tariq entered the lounge, glancing back over his shoulder at Dave, who was making his way up the stairs.

Tariq saw the first clock; it was on the mantel piece above the downstairs fire place. How was he going to get that?

THUD, DONK, CLANK, DONK, PING, DONK, THUD.

The noise set Tariq shaking, what on earth was that? He poked his head out of the lounge and saw a broken clock lying at the bottom of the stairs.

Phew, he thought, *that must've been Dave's first clock.*

Back to the task at hand.

Tariq noticed a wheelie footstool in the middle of the lounge floor and nudged it towards the fire place. Jumping on to it he reached for the clock and sent it spinning towards the floor.

Excellent, he thought, that was his first one. Feeling much better he looked around the rest of the room. No more in here; time to move to the next room.

Into the dining room he went.

"Oh my god," Tariq exclaimed as he looked up at the huge pendulum clock. The clock was attached to the dining room wall; it was a good one and a half metres above the floor. *How on earth am I going to get that?* He said to himself.

THUD, DONK, CLANK, DONK, PING, DONK, THUD.

Tariq dived into his shell.

"Oi," said Shell, "What are you playing at? You know I will leave you don't you?"

"Shell this just isn't the time or the place. OK?" Tariq said to Shell.

"Why are we here? This isn't our hutch. Are you doing something you shouldn't?" Shell continued.

"Just don't. OK. I've no time to explain," Tariq said.

"Just don't what?" Shell demanded.

"Shell, please, I'll explain later, but not just now. OK?"

"Do you really think you can put me off that easily?" Shell said.

"Shell... Please... I'm trying to do something important," Tariq said.

Shell started laughing "Important? You? Are you kidding?"

"NO. I AM NOT," Tariq said firmly.

Shell was more than slightly shocked at Tariq's tone.

"You really are trying to do something important then?" Shell said.

"Yes."

"Really?" Shell asked once more, trying to make sure Tariq was.

"YES," Tariq said again.

"Ok. Tell me later," Shell said.

"OK. I will. Can I get on now?" Tariq said in a manner which meant he would not take an answer that said not.

"I suppose so," said Shell.

Tariq reached into his satchel and pulled out a couple of heavy duty springs.

I think these may do the trick, Tariq said to himself as he attached the springs to his feet.

Once they were on he started to bounce.

"Please forgive me Shell."

Tariq was leaping up and down and when he had reached the right speed he aimed himself at the wall clock. Just before making contact with it he retreated into his shell.

CRUNCH.

He hit the clock full force.

TWANG, CRACK, SMASH.

The clock came away from the wall and landed on the floor.

"Ouch," said Shell.

"It didn't hurt that much Shell. Stop whinging," Shell didn't say anything else.

Tariq was over the moon; what a success. The only problem he had now was how he was going to stop himself bouncing around the room.

After bouncing off the floor for the fifty millionth time he managed to reach one of his feet, whilst he was in mid-air, and dislodge one of the springs.

Tremendous. he thought. Then realising he was going to hit the floor with only one spring he changed his mind and thought, *OH NO*.

He hit the floor hard, on his only remaining spring, then bounced off the floor at a strange angle and zoomed through the air cart wheeling like a carrot that had been used as a Frisbee.

This was going to get a bit bumpy. Tariq retreated back into his shell once again and held on tightly. The only thing that was left to be seen, on the outside of his shell, was the remaining spring. After bumping into the odd bits of furniture around the room Tariq eventually came to a spinning halt.

He popped his head and arms out of Shell and removed the final spring.

Hmm, he thought, *probably not the best decision I've ever made.*

Tariq moved the remnants of the clock into the kitchen.

After getting rid of the remaining clocks in the lounge and the dining room, all that was left to do was the kitchen.

On the oven and the microwave there were the usual digital clocks. He got both of these by loading some broken bits and pieces from the other room onto the spring, pulling back and letting it go. The bits of broken furniture and clock from the lounge hit the oven's display, smashing it.

Although broken, the remains of the oven's digital display was sparking as the electricity short circuited within it.

Tariq checked the kitchen cupboards one by one, each of them was empty. But when he opened the last one there was a most peculiar looking grey box-like clock. It had a red hand, it had a black hand, and it had grey tubes attached to it. He knew that this was the last clock he would have to deal with and it didn't matter that it was a strange one.

Tariq pulled it, he heaved it, and he pushed it. The clock was not going to give way. He made one final attempt by wedging a spatula, one he had found in a cupboard, between the grey clock and the wall. After a great effort he managed to unfix it. The clock with the red and black hands came away and Tariq was relieved.

Then a loud and angry hissing sound started. He moved back quickly from the cupboard and looked in. All Tariq could see, in the dim light of the cupboard, was some kind of greyish ribbed snake with its mouth open in a big 'O' shape, hissing at him.

"Snakes!" Tariq screamed, he didn't like snakes one bit, he had to find Dave. Dave would know what to do.

Tariq scarpered from the kitchen faster than a tortoise on springs and made his way to the stairs and looked up at the incredibly steep slope.

Tariq's heart sunk. *Oh my god*, he thought and paused.

Hearing the hissing once again and smelling an awful, awful rotten egg smell which came from it, he quickly legged it up the stairs. It was only when he reached the top he wondered how he had managed it.

"Dave, Dave, there's something really wrong. The clock had a snake in it. A snake can you believe that?" Tariq said to Dave.

"What are you going on about Tariq? Snakes in clocks? You must be mistaken."

"No, no," Tariq replied.

Tariq was looking worse than Dave had ever seen him before, paler than pale.

"Don't worry Tariq. Only one more clock up here on the mantel piece to sort out, once I've dealt with that, I'll go down and have a look for you," Dave said, trying to calm Tariq.

"Thanks, Dave," Tariq said, relieved that Dave seemed to have everything under control.

They crossed the room to the fire place; Tariq could now help Dave to reach the final clock which was perched on the mantel piece.

Chapter 20.
Gas

The grey gas meter with the red and black hands was off the wall and hissing, spilling gas out at an incredible rate. Gradually the kitchen was filled with the gas; all the while the oven's display was crackling with electrical sparks.

Inch by inch the fumes filled the kitchen from the floor up; wafting towards the oven's broken display.

All of a sudden, with one huge BOOM, the Emit's house suddenly and loudly re-arranged itself into a badly stacked pile of bricks and rubble as the gas caught light and exploded.

A large piece of brick crashed on to the drain where the Time Goblin had been staying all this time. It smashed through the cover and hit the Time Goblin squarely on the head. The goblin's life force was bashed out of it and it promptly turned back into the mud and slime from which it was made.

All that was left standing, of the Emit's house, was the chimney stack and where the second floor had been only the hearth of the fireplace remained. On this Dave and Tariq stood looking at each other, quite surprised.

"Oh," Tariq said to Dave.

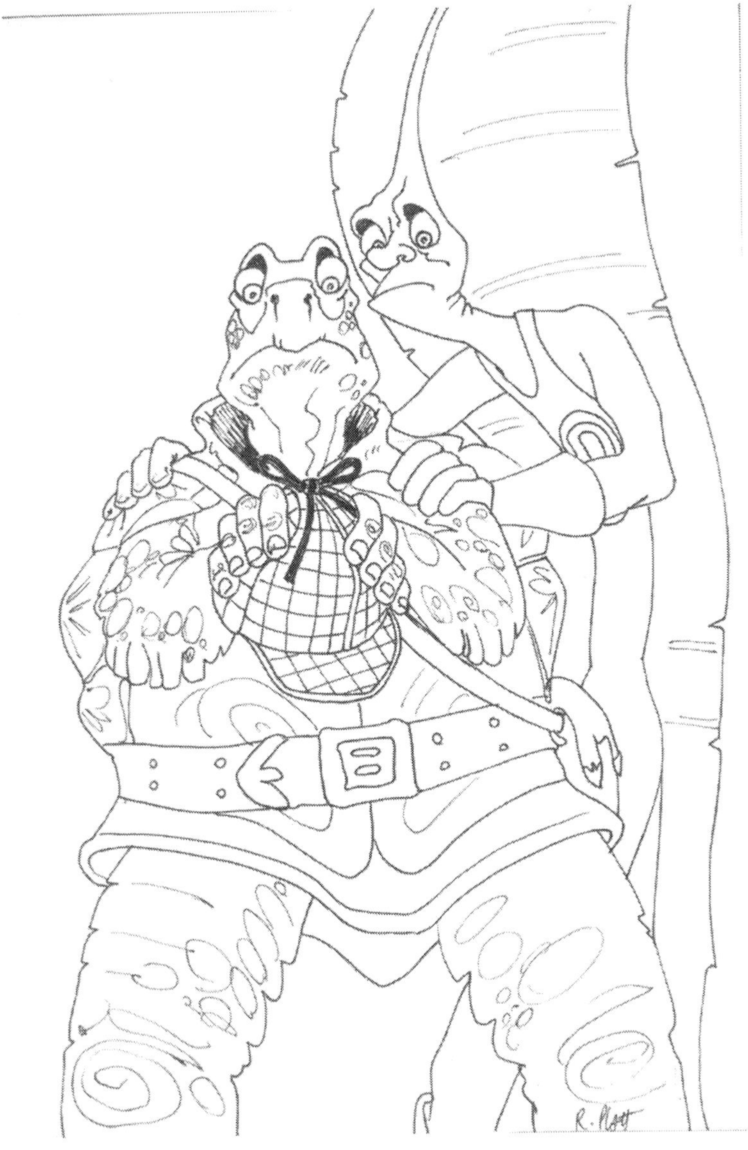
R. Platt

"Oh," Dave agreed.

"Well, we got rid of the clocks then," Tariq said trying to put what had happened in the best possible light.

"Yeah," replied Dave, still totally gobsmacked.

"Quite a good view really, once you get rid of the walls," Tariq said.

"I suppose it is, really," Dave said.

"D'you think they'll notice?" Tariq said thinking of the Emits and the dog.

"Well, I suppose we could suggest that it was some kind of make over by Changing Rooms or something."

"What?" Tariq said.

"No I didn't buy that either," Dave was gradually coming out of his shock.

Without the walls of the house Dave and Tariq were now exposed to the elements. The wind was gusting and Dave was having some trouble remaining on the hearth.

"Oh great," Dave exclaimed as he noticed that his trolley was now exposed and the hedge seemed to have got up and left at some stage. "I never got to wear my shell suit."

"Seventh. Is that you?"

Dave looked from left to right. Who was calling him by his old name? It certainly wasn't Tariq.

"It is you," said Jonesy, as he flew down to the chimney stack. "I was wondering where you had got to."

"Jonesy, what are you doing here?" Dave asked.

"Some problem with the holiday lake not being finished; what. Couldn't really understand what they were trying to say. Decided to come back. Who's this?" Jonesy said looking at Tariq.

"That's Tariq. He's been helping me to do some amazing things," Dave said.

"It's good to hear you haven't been wasting your time since you left us. I like the chimney stack. Reminds me of a pile of bricks I was once acquainted with," Jonesy said.

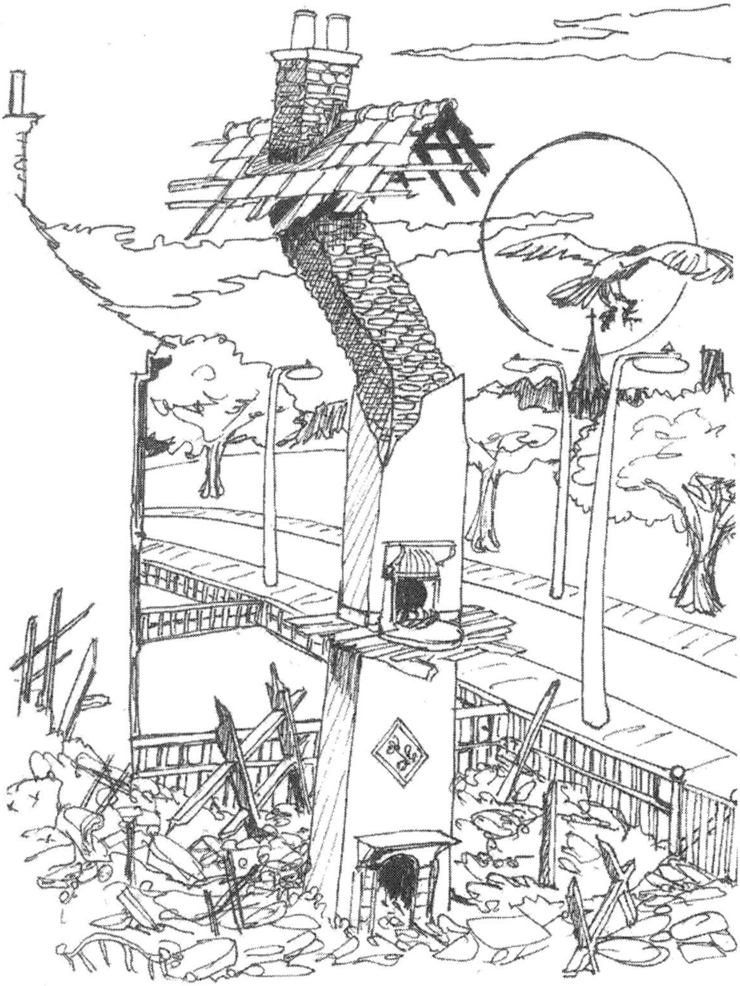

Dave surveyed the remains of the Emit's house. From their vantage point, one floor up and no walls, Dave could see the park where the Emits had taken the dog for a walk, which was not strictly true as it was where the dog had gone to take the Emits for a walk.

Worryingly Dave saw that the dog and the Emits were making their way back.

"Jonesy, I don't suppose you could give me and Tariq a lift could you?"

"Anything for you young sir," Jonesy said.

"We need to go over there," Dave said, pointing to Tariq's hutch which was at the back of a house a couple of blocks up the road.

"OK, grab hold."

"Thanks Jonesy."

With that Tariq and Dave grabbed hold of a claw each and Jonesy swooshed his huge wings. Up and away they went towards Tariq's home.

Chapter 21.
Dogs Don't Like Rubble

The dog scampered up the road ahead of Trevor and Daphne and was just about to turn into their house when it tripped over a brick.

The dog picked itself up to carry on up the path when all of a sudden its back legs gave way. The dog just sat and stared.

"OH MY DOG!" the dog said. "How stupid was I to think that that crazy feather could stop my nervous tick? He's destroyed my master's home. If I ever see him again..."

"Oh Trevor," said Daphne as she reached the entrance to what used to be their house. "Aren't we lucky?"

Trevor's chin nearly hit the floor, twice, once because his lovely home was now just a pile of rubble and the second time, because for some inexplicable reason, Daphne thought they were lucky. The shock must have got to her he thought.

"Why are we lucky? Our house has gone, it's been — totally destroyed," said Trevor trying to grasp the enormity of the situation.

"We're lucky because of the dog," Daphne said.

"Because of the dog?" Trevor asked, utterly astounded by his wife's comment, "Because the dog is alive?" he said, trying to understand.

"No. Because the dog must have known something was going to happen. It got us out of the house didn't it?" his wife replied.

"I suppose you're right," said Trevor, but he didn't feel lucky, he had no job and no way of ever buying another house, and Daphne didn't know he hadn't been keeping up the insurance payments on their home, because he was not earning any money. He was sure she would leave him, when she found out this little titbit of information.

Trevor had had enough. What a miserable life he had had and to bring Daphne into it as well.

If only I could click my fingers just like this and turn back time, Trevor thought as he clicked his fingers, hoping beyond hope that everything would be alright and not knowing he was a Time Guardian without a Time Goblin to do battle with.

Chapter 22.
No Problem

Morning was breaking it was 7:14 a.m. Trevor opened his eyes; he had been roused by the *click, click, click,* of a bicycle freewheeling. It was the postman.

The postman rested his bicycle against the front garden's wall and walked up the path to the front door. Putting his hand into his post bag he pulled out a single letter and shoved it into the letter box. The letter box was one of those you sometimes see attached to the front of the house, one which had to be opened from the outside.

The postman got back on his bike and cycled off to the next address requiring a delivery.

Trevor got up, went down the stairs, opened the front door and retrieved the letter.

The dog came out from the back of the house and wandered round to the front, as if to see whether Trevor would manage to get the letter.

The tick peeked out from the hair on the dogs head and started to feel relaxed.

"Relaxed," It said to itself. This was certainly a new sensation. There was no sign of that horrid little green man and its horrid nasty wooden frame. Perhaps the tick didn't need to try and leave after all.

After double checking once more that the coast was clear and that there really was no sign of the horrid little green man, the tick pulled up its deck chair and sat back to read its favourite book by H.G. Wells; the Time Machine.

Trevor opened the letter, read it, and looked at where he thought he had a watch.

"Strange, I thought I had one," Trevor muttered to himself and then thought; *somehow this all seems vaguely familiar.*

Trevor walked through his house looking for a clock. He couldn't find one anywhere and actually he felt he really didn't need one.

"Trevor what does the letter say?" Daphne called down from upstairs.

"It says I need to turn up at the new job by 10:15am."

"What's the time now?" she asked.

"7:33am and 24 seconds" Trevor said, automatically and then frowned, whilst covering his now gaping mouth with his hand. He had a little think. *Where did that come from?* He thought further.

"At least that gives you plenty of time to get ready then," said Daphne.

"Yeah, it does. Do you fancy taking the dog for a walk?" Trevor said to his wife.

About the Author

After working consistently in I.T. for 27 years I decided it was time to forego the strictly logical world of computing and take up writing in my spare time. I don't think I'll ever truly get to grips with this literary world but I'm certainly having great fun finding out about it, though I think my wife, Yve, is not so enamoured by my frequent requests asking 'what do you think of this?'

That said, without her, I don't think my three

children's books would have ever seen the light of day and I wouldn't have enough stuff to be able to have my very own website created — www.srwoodward.co.uk.

Other Brave Dave books;

Brave Dave and The Time Goblin

Brave Dave and The Caribbean Conspiracy

Coming very, very soon;

Brave Dave and The Space Oddity

www.BraveDave.co.uk

www.srwoodward.co.uk

Made in the USA
Charleston, SC
17 October 2014